THE PUZZLE CLUB™
POISON-PEN MYSTERY

by Dandi Daley Mackall

Based on characters developed for *The Puzzle Club Christmas Mystery*, an original story by Mark Young for Lutheran Hour Ministries

Lutheran Hour
Ministries

CPH.
SAINT LOUIS

Puzzle Club™ Mysteries
The Puzzle Club Christmas Mystery
The Puzzle Club Mystery of Great Price
The Puzzle Club Case of the Kidnapped Kid
The Puzzle Club Poison-Pen Mystery

Cover illustration by Mike Young Productions

Scripture quotations taken from the HOLY BIBLE, NEW INTERNATIONAL VERSION®. NIV®. Copyright © 1973, 1978, 1984 by International Bible Society. Used by permission of Zondervan Publishing House. All rights reserved.

Copyright © 1998 International Lutheran Laymen's League

™ Trademark of International Lutheran Laymen's League

Published by Concordia Publishing House
3558 S. Jefferson Avenue, St. Louis, MO 63118-3968
Manufactured in the United States of America

1 2 3 4 5 6 7 8 9 10   07 06 05 04 03 02 01 00 99 98

Contents

1

First Strike

"The Puzzle Club meeting will begin!" Tobias said, calling Christopher, Korina, and Alex to attention. "This is serious business. Everything has to be perfect."

Tobias paced the floor of his puzzle shop. Alex had never seen their friend so nervous. Tobias had called each of them at home and asked everyone to meet him at Puzzleworks before he opened the store.

Alex tried to look as alert as Korina and Christopher, but he didn't feel alert. Wasn't an 11-year-old kid supposed to be able to sleep late during his first week of summer vacation?

"Alex," said Tobias, running his fingers through his white hair, "are you listening?" His voice was sharper than Alex had ever heard it.

Alex swallowed his yawn. "I'm listening," he said.

Korina sighed and shook her head. "Please continue, Tobias," she said. "*Christopher* and *I* are listening."

Alex hated it when Korina tried to leave him out of The Puzzle Club's business. Korina was only 13. Christopher, who was 14, never tried to leave Alex out of things. Alex took out his notebook to show he was on the job every bit as much as Korina.

Tobias fumbled with the puzzle pieces strewn on his counter. Tobias' Puzzleworks store had puzzles everywhere—on shelves, in racks, in the window. Tobias motioned for them to sit in the puzzle corner. Beanbag chairs surrounded a giant jigsaw puzzle—about halfway assembled—that lay on the floor.

"An old, old friend is coming to town today," Tobias said.

"For the centennial, Tobias?" Christopher asked. It was the city's one hundredth birthday. The mayor was seeing to it that everybody celebrated the event.

"P-P-Perhaps ... in a way," Tobias said, stuttering in his excitement. "His name was ... is ... R-R-Randy. R-R-Randy R-R-Randolph."

6

"So what's the matter with him?" Alex asked.

"Nothing!" Tobias shot back. "There's nothing wrong with R-R-Randy Randolph."

Alex felt like he should apologize, but he did not know for what. "But ... why does everything have to be perfect?" he asked.

"It just does," Tobias said. "He hasn't been back here for a long time."

"How long, Tobias?" Christopher asked. He was loading a new roll of film into his camera.

"Ah, let's see now," Tobias said, stirring the unused puzzle pieces on the floor. "Must be 25 ... no, more like 35 years."

"Thirty-five years?" Alex repeated. "He must be as old as you!"

"Real nice, Alex," Korina said.

"As president of The Puzzle Club," Christopher said, "I speak for all of us. We're here to help. What do you need us to do?"

"Thank you, Christopher," Tobias said, sounding relieved. "And you too, Korina and Alex. Mr. Randolph will probably stay with his daughter-in-law and granddaughter while he's in town. His son died a while back." Tobias fell silent for a minute.

Tobias started pacing again. "I'm hoping we can convince Mr. Randolph to come back and live here. I've invited him for dinner tonight. I need you three to do some shopping for me."

"No problem," Christopher said. He took the shopping list Tobias held out to him.

"Just remember," Tobias said. "Everything has to be perfect."

Christopher divided the list and gave Korina and Alex their assignments.

Korina frowned at her list. "It's not exactly detective work," she said after Tobias had moved to the back of the shop.

"Korina," said Christopher, "after all Tobias does for us, this is the least we can do for him."

"Yeah, Korina," Alex said. He studied his list. Stamps. Tons of groceries. "Christopher, I won't be able to carry all of this."

"Okay, Alex," Christopher said. "I'll meet you at the market after I check the bus schedule for Tobias." Korina was already out the door as Alex and Christopher left Puzzleworks.

Alex squinted at the sun as he headed for the post office. He walked with his head down, letting his eyes get used to the brightness. Alex was still looking at the sidewalk when he reached the post office. He climbed the stairs to the entrance.

Thump! Alex felt a shove that threw him off balance as someone stormed out of the

8

post office. The push nearly knocked him down the stairs.

"Hey!" he yelled. "What's the big idea?" Alex looked up into the round face of his old kindergarten teacher, Miss Jones. Although she wasn't that much taller than Alex, she probably weighed three times as much as he did. No wonder he'd almost been knocked over.

"*Big* idea?" Miss Jones asked. "Did you say 'What's the *big* idea?' I get it. Very funny. Very, very funny, indeed." Tears rolled down over her chubby, red cheeks.

"Miss Jones?" Alex said. "I'm sorry. I didn't know it was you."

His old teacher glared at him. She shook a letter she clutched in her right hand. "How dare you!" she said through her teeth. "How dare any of you! You think I don't *know* I'm f-f-fat?" Then she crumpled her letter with both hands, wadded it into a ball, and threw it into a thornbush. Without another word, she clomped down the post office steps.

Alex stared after Miss Jones. He felt as if he'd come in on the tail end of a nightmare. He'd always thought Miss Jones kind of liked him when he was in kindergarten. What could he have done to make her so mad after all these years? He did remember cracking jokes with some of the other kids about her weight. But he hadn't meant to hurt her feelings.

Alex got Tobias' stamps and walked to Hales Market to meet Christopher. He spotted Korina talking to Mr. Rafferty, the park maintenance man. Mr. Rafferty stood partway up a ladder, holding a big banner in one hand. It read "Centennial: 100 Years of Excellence." The other end of the banner was tied to the biggest tree in the town square.

Alex waved, but Korina and Mr. Rafferty didn't seem to notice him. They were arguing about something. Mr. Rafferty kept shaking a piece of paper in Korina's face. She looked as puzzled as Alex had felt when Miss Jones had yelled at *him*.

It seemed cool in Hales Market. Alex let the screen door slam behind him.

"Who's that?" yelled Mr. Hales. "I hear you."

It wasn't Mr. Hales' usual welcome. "It's me, Mr. Hales. Alex."

"Well, what are you standing there for?" Mr. Hales looked Alex over from head to toe. "What are you doing here?" he barked.

Alex decided this just wasn't his day. "I'm only getting things from my list," he said. He finally found it in his back pocket. "I'm picking up some things for Tobias."

Alex took a small basket and walked down the grocery aisle. He sensed Mr. Hales watching him every step of the way. Mr. Hales wasn't acting as friendly as he usually was.

The little bell rang, alerting Mr. Hales to another customer. Alex felt relieved. Maybe Mr. Hales would stare at somebody else.

Alex heard Christopher's voice. "… just getting them for Tobias. Are you okay, Mr. Hales?"

So it wasn't just Alex. "Christopher," Alex called, "I'm over here." The boys gathered everything Tobias had asked for—tomato sauce, tomatoes, rigatoni, lettuce, cheese. They waited in line while the man ahead of them bought a case of cola.

"And that's a fair price on the case," Mr. Hales said. "Anyone who says otherwise is a liar." The man didn't answer. He grabbed his carton and walked briskly out of Hales Market.

Mr. Hales totaled the items Christopher and Alex had collected. "Wow," Christopher said, taking out the money Tobias had given him. "I didn't think it would be that much."

Mr. Hales slapped the counter. A loud crack echoed through the store. "My prices are as fair as anybody's in town! Fairer!" he yelled.

Christopher stared, wide-eyed, at the store owner. "I know, Mr. Hales. I didn't mean …"

"Get out of my store!" Mr. Hales hollered. "Right now! Get out! And take your money with you!"

"But …" Christopher said.

"Out!"

Christopher picked up Tobias' money off the counter. A piece of paper floated to the floor. Alex leaned down and picked it up. The letter had been crumpled, leaving it so wrinkled it was hard to read. But as he set it back on the counter, Alex caught enough to figure out why Mr. Hales was so angry. *You cheat!* it read. And something about *unfair prices—going to be sorry* and *get even.*

"What was that about?" Christopher asked once they were safely out of Hales Market.

Alex told Christopher what he'd been able to make out in the letter. "What's it mean, Christopher?" he asked.

"I'm not sure, Alex," Christopher said. "But I think Mr. Hales is the victim of a poison-pen letter.

2

The Cruel Case

"What's a poison-pen letter?" Alex asked.

"It's a cruel kind of note or letter," Christopher explained. "Someone writes a letter to hurt another person as much as possible. That's why it's called *poison*."

They had to walk two blocks to another grocery store. Alex had time to think about the morning. "That's it!" he declared. "I'll bet Miss Jones got a poison letter ..."

"Poison-*pen* letter," Christopher corrected.

"Yeah. That's why she was so mad at me," Alex said. "It must have said something about her being fat. Who would write a poison-pen letter, Christopher?"

"That's just it," Christopher explained. "The writers don't usually sign their names."

Christopher and Alex went about the business of gathering Tobias' groceries. This time the bill was almost three dollars higher than at Hales Market. They walked out of the store, each lugging two bags full of groceries.

"I wish I'd gotten a look at Mr. Hales' letter," Christopher said. "Nobody should be allowed to send those things. Maybe I'd have noticed a clue."

"I'm not about to ask Mr. Hales to see it," Alex said. "But I'll bet you could see Miss Jones' note. She threw it in a thornbush by the post office."

"Then let's not waste time around here!" Christopher said. He took off running as if his arms were free.

Alex trotted after him. A bag of apples toppled out of his grocery bag. He stuffed it back in and hoped Tobias planned to make applesauce. Finally, Alex reached the post office. He was out of breath.

Christopher hollered at him from the post office steps. "Where is it, Alex?"

Alex set his bag down beside Christopher's. He was glad Tobias hadn't wanted ice cream. The sun beat down so hot that the concrete steps felt warm. He showed Christopher the thornbush on the north side of the post office.

"That's where Miss Jones hurled the note," he said.

"Hmmmm," Christopher said. "I think I see it down there, but I'm afraid I'm too big to reach in and get it." He turned and grinned at Alex.

Alex sighed. "What I won't do for The Puzzle Club," he said.

"And for your old kindergarten teacher," Christopher added.

"Out of my way!" screamed an old man with bushy eyebrows. He tore down the post office steps.

"Mr. Willakers," Christopher said, stepping out of his way. "Are you okay?"

"Like you'd care," he said. "Scoot!" He shook his fist at the boys. Alex saw the letter he clutched in his hand.

"Christopher," Alex whispered as Mr. Willakers thundered off, "did you see …?"

"Another poison-pen letter, I'd imagine," Christopher said. He'd just gotten the words out when a high squeal made them turn toward the post office door. The noise, which sounded like a train throwing on its brakes, came from inside. Seconds later a tall, thin woman ran out. She held one hand over her mouth. Her other hand gripped a letter. Tears streamed down her cheeks.

"Alex," Christopher said, "find that letter!"

Alex lowered himself off the side of the post office steps. He squeezed through the little hole in the thornbush. The minty, piney smell of the nearby evergreens made him think of Christmas. Branches scratched his bare legs and arms. "I see it!" Alex called to Christopher.

Alex managed to reach the paper with his foot. He slid it forward until it was close enough to grab. Then he handed it up to Christopher.

"What are you doing down there?" Korina sounded like she was accusing him of something. She must have finished her errand and seen Christopher on the post office steps.

Evergreen branches and thorns pressed all around him. Alex was starting to feel like a caterpillar locked in a cocoon. "Tell Christopher to give me a hand," he told Korina.

Instead, Korina stretched her hand down. Alex took hold. He stuck one foot up on the step and let Korina pull. She may have been a girl, but she sure was strong.

16

Christopher was already taking pictures of the note. "It's a poison-pen letter that Miss Jones received," he explained to Korina. "Mr. Hales got one too. And from what we've seen around here, I don't think he and Miss Jones are the only victims."

Korina pulled out her magnifying glass and examined the note. "This looks like the kind of paper Mr. Rafferty had. He kept yelling at me and demanding I tell him who sent it. He even thought *I* had sent it. He must have gotten a poison-pen letter too."

Alex moved in to read the note. It said: *To Miss Fatty Jones, the fattest teacher in the world. You should quit because everybody is sick of looking at you.* The message had been printed in capital letters written to look like a child's printing.

"Poor Miss Jones," Alex said. "No wonder she was so upset." He wished he would have said something nicer to her. And even though he'd been only 5 years old in kindergarten when he'd laughed at her behind her back, he wished he hadn't done that either.

"Miss Jones has taught here for years," Korina said. "She taught my father. She's older than Tobias."

Christopher folded the note and stuck it into his pocket. "We'll need to get this to headquarters and analyze it," he said. "In the meantime, we'd better get back to Puzzleworks. Tobias will be worried."

Alex felt like his groceries were getting heavier and heavier as they walked to Puzzleworks. When they were still half a block away, Alex heard loud voices coming from inside the store. Someone was griping loud and clear.

"And Betty Jenkins," the voice roared, "she would be late to her own funeral! We had to wait nearly an hour. Jeff Monroe's got to be the world's worst carpenter. You'd think in a hundred years the town could have come up with someone who could build a simple speaker's platform for ..."

Korina opened the door to Puzzleworks. Christopher and Alex carried the groceries inside. It took a minute for Alex's eyes to adjust to the dimness inside after the bright sunshine outdoors. When they did adjust, Alex saw Tobias talking with two men and a young girl with wavy, blonde hair. He recognized the man talking as the mayor.

Tobias called to them. "Come, come," he said. "These are the people I wanted you to

18

meet. Mayor, I think you're familiar with The Puzzle Club—Christopher, Korina, and Alex."

"Sheriff Grimaldi has told me a lot about you," said the mayor. "You're a lot younger than I thought you'd be, though." He shook Chris-topher's hand.

"How do you do?" Christopher said.

"Not so well at present," said the mayor. "Our big celebration in the square is less than a week away. I am surrounded by incompetents. Why, just this morning that Mr. Willakers ..."

Tobias interrupted him. "Excuse me, Mayor. I need to introduce The Puzzle Club to my old friend. Randy, these are the ones I was telling you about. Alex, Korina, Christopher, I'd like you to meet Mr. Randolph, an old and dear friend. And this is his granddaughter ..."

"Micki, right?" Korina said. "I thought I recognized you. You were in my social studies class last year. Remember?"

"I think I've seen you in the library," Christopher said to Micki.

"Probably," Korina said. "As you know, I do a great deal of research in the library. I think Micki spends even more time there than I do."

Micki nodded without looking up. She pressed a little closer to her grandfather.

"Miss Micki is proving of great service to me in our centennial celebration," said the mayor.

"My granddaughter has been volunteering her time at the mayor's office. It really surprised her mother." Mr. Randolph put his arm around his granddaughter. "You might say Micki isn't the most talkative gal in town."

Alex happened to look at Tobias. He was surprised by what he saw. Instead of wearing his usual, jolly smile, he seemed tired and sad. Alex knew Tobias had been looking forward to seeing his friend again. So why did Tobias look as if he might cry at any minute?

No sooner had Alex asked himself the question, than he got his answer. Tobias had something wadded up in his hand—something that looked to Alex exactly like a poison-pen letter.

3

Poison Prevention

Alex was dying to know what was in Tobias' poison-pen letter. He couldn't imagine anybody finding one mean word to say about Tobias. Tobias loved Jesus so much, it seemed to overflow to everyone he met.

"Then there's Alfred Barney." The mayor's voice droned on about somebody else. "That man doesn't know the meaning of hard work. How he ever got on the centennial committee is beyond me." The mayor stopped and patted Micki on the head. "Young Micki here is a different story. She's just about the best worker I have."

Micki shrugged, but Mr. Randolph grinned from ear to ear. Alex hadn't noticed before how old Mr. Randolph looked—older than Tobias. And his face wasn't smooth like Tobias', but crusty and leathery looking. Instead of little lines at the corners of his eyes, Mr. Randolph's lines looked like hundreds of deep streams.

The mayor started up another complaint. "Teasdale, the concrete fellow, he ..."

Alex couldn't wait another minute. "Tobias, could I see you for a minute?"

"Alex," Tobias said, "can't it wait? I have company."

"I'm sorry, Tobias," Alex said. "It's really important. I can't wait."

Tobias excused himself, though the mayor didn't seem to notice. He hadn't missed a beat. "...lumpy concrete, and no wood to speak of, I ..."

Tobias and Alex stepped over to the set of shelves that hid the entrance to Puzzle Club headquarters.

"Well, Alex?" Tobias asked, his face sad. His eyes lacked even a hint of their usual twinkle.

"Tobias," Alex whispered, "what did *yours* say?"

"Alex," Tobias said, "what are you talking about?"

"Your letter," Alex said.

Tobias looked at the letter still in his hand. He jerked his hand behind his back. He gulped. "W-W-What …"

"Tobias," Alex said, "I know it must say something mean. But whatever it says, it's not true."

"What do you know about this, Alex?" Tobias asked.

"I don't know anything about it. Except you're not the only one who got one. It *is* a mean letter, isn't it? A poison-pen letter?"

"W-W-Why, I suppose it is a poison-pen letter. But how could you possibly know?" Tobias shook his head. His white hair fell across his forehead and he brushed it back. "You Puzzle Club detectives are amazing. The mailman delivered this right after you left this morning."

Alex thought he saw tears in Tobias' eyes. Alex felt a lump the size of a potato in his own throat. "Tobias, I don't ever want to know what that horrible note says. But you have to believe that whatever it says, it's a lie. You're the best person I know. You've taught me more about Jesus than anybody in the world. You said He loved us enough to die for us. No mean letter can take that kind of love away."

Tobias leaned down and gave Alex a quick hug. "Thank you, Alex," he said, the old Tobias grin returning. "I guess I needed to hear that."

Tobias took the note from behind his back. He wadded it into a ball and dropped it into the wastebasket. Alex started to ask for the note— it was a clue. Then he decided against it. Whatever that note said, nobody else needed to read it.

"Alex," Tobias said, "what did you mean when you said I wasn't the only one to receive that letter?"

"Not *that* letter exactly," Alex explained. "But we know of three or four people who received poison-pen letters this morning. And I have a feeling a lot more people than that got poisoned."

"Other people?" Tobias asked.

"Yeah. The notes say stuff like you're fat or you're a cheat. That's why they call them poison," Alex said.

"This is terrible!" Tobias said. "What if Randy …" He stopped speaking, as if the words were too awful to say out loud.

"I know you wanted everything to be perfect for Mr. Randolph," Alex said, "but I don't see why this would bother him."

"No," Tobias said. "You wouldn't understand. You have to stop this, Alex. Randy Randolph *cannot* receive a poison-pen letter!"

"Why would he get one, Tobias?" Alex asked. Then he thought about it. If Tobias could get one, anybody could.

"Alex," Tobias said, pulling at his hair so hard Alex was afraid he'd pull it out, "you and The Puzzle Club had better solve this poison-pen mystery *fast*—before my friend gets a letter like I did. Trust me, Alex. You can't let that happen."

Alex and Tobias joined the others. The mayor was walking toward the door. "Ah, there you are, Tobias. Well, we'll see you later."

"Nice to meet you, Mayor," said Mr. Randolph.

"Yes, yes, of course," returned the mayor. He turned when the reporter from the *Daily Record* walked by outside. "You there!" the mayor called, running down the street after the reporter.

"Whew," Mr. Randolph said softly. "Let's see. Where were we, Tobias, before the storm blew in?"

Tobias chuckled. "The mayor can be a bit blustery," he said. "You had just started telling me what really brought you back to our fair city."

Mr. Randolph smiled down at Micki. "I figured it was time to get to know my granddaughter. She and my daughter-in-law have had to make a go of it alone long enough, I expect."

"I couldn't agree with you more," Tobias said. "So you'll come to dinner? Bring Sally too. The kids bought plenty." He motioned toward the grocery bags still sitting on the floor. "Six o'clock."

"Six it is," Mr. Randolph answered. He and Micki started out the door. Then Mr. Randolph stopped. "What would you say if my granddaughter spent the afternoon with The Puzzle Club?"

"No, Grandpa," Micki said. "I don't want to."

"Come on now, girl," he said, "don't be shy." He looked to Tobias. "Far as I can tell, Micki doesn't have any friends of her own. It's been six months since she and her mother moved here from the country. Sally had to look for work. She's cleaning houses. That's how she

26

and Micki met up with the mayor. She does his house on Tuesdays."

"Hey, Micki," Alex said, "if you stick around, you can help out. We've got this big case ..."

Korina's elbow in his side stopped Alex in mid-sentence. Then he remembered. Detective Rule Number 7: *Keep all Puzzle Club cases strictly private.*

"That's fine then," said Mr. Randolph. "Have fun, Micki. See you at six, Tobias." And he left. Micki looked like she wanted to stay about as much as Korina wanted her to stay.

"So what do we do with her, Christopher?" Korina whispered loud enough for Micki to hear.

"Micki," Christopher said, "how'd you like to hang out with Alex for awhile? Korina and I have some investigations and experiments to conduct."

"Are you really detectives?" Micki asked.

"We sure are!" Alex said. "The Puzzle Club detectives. That's us."

"Alex can tell you all about it," Christopher said. "He's one of our best detectives."

Korina laughed out loud. When she'd stopped laughing long enough to talk, she said, "Old Alex the Detective can tell you about all the cases he's cracked. Meanwhile, Christopher and I have some *real* detective work to take care of."

Sherlock, The Puzzle Club's parakeet mascot, flew in and landed on Alex's shoulder.

"What is it?" Micki asked.

"It's not an *it*," Alex said. "This is Sherlock, the smartest parakeet in the world."

"That's true," Korina said. "He's so smart, he's a better detective than Alex."

"Sherlock," said Alex, ignoring Korina, "this is Micki."

"*Braawk! Micki!*" said Sherlock. Then he flew off Alex's shoulder and landed on Micki's.

Alex had never seen Sherlock take to strangers before. "Well, that's a new one!" he said. "I think Sherlock likes you, Micki."

"So," Christopher said, "I guess we'll see you guys later."

Alex knew Christopher and Korina wanted him to take Micki outside. They wanted to examine the poison-pen letter more closely. "Okay," he said. "We're going now."

Alex said good-bye to Tobias and walked outside with Micki. "Wait here just a minute," he said when they got to the curb outside

Puzzleworks. "Talk to Sherlock. I'll be right back." Alex dashed back inside.

"What are you doing back here, Alex?" Korina asked.

"I need a few things," he said, rushing past her and Christopher. "I have my own investigating to do." He pulled the thick, gold cord behind Tobias' counter. A shelf of puzzles on one wall slid back to reveal a secret, arched doorway. Alex ran through the doorway and took the stairs up to the attic two at a time.

When he got to the top of the stairs, Alex had one hand on the doorknob when he remembered the security alarm. If he didn't punch in the secret code, bells and alarms would sound. It wouldn't be the first time he'd set off the alarm, but not this time.

"Alex!" Korina yelled up at him. "Don't forget to punch in the code."

"I didn't forget," he yelled back, punching in the code.

"Sure you didn't, Alex," Korina said. It made Alex fume. He *had* remembered. Why did Korina always have to think she was so much more brilliant than he was?

Alex pushed straight through headquarters, past Korina's latest invention, which looked like a robot to Alex. He bumped the examination table and heard Christopher's developing solution slosh out, but he didn't have time to clean it up. Alex ran straight to his clothes rack. As master of disguises, Alex had collected costumes and clothing for every need.

Alex fingered through the army uniform, trench coat, clown costume, and women's dresses until he found exactly what he wanted. His mail carrier's uniform. He rolled it up and stuck it into a brown bag. Just let Korina wonder what he was up to. Alex passed Christopher and Korina on his way down the stairs.

"Take your time, Alex," Korina said. "Christopher and I are on the case. We'll get to the bottom of the poison-pen mystery."

"Oh yeah?" Alex yelled back. "Not if I get there first."

4

Mail Mystery

Alex and Micki hadn't been on the street for five minutes before Alex knew the poison was spreading. Two older couples passed each other on the sidewalk in front of Puzzleworks.

"What are you staring at?" one of the men yelled.

"What are *you* staring at?" the other man shot back.

"Don't you yell at my husband!" said the one woman.

"Don't you yell at *my* husband," said the other woman. Then both couples hurried away, grumbling at each other.

"*Braawk! Fight!*" Sherlock said. He covered his face with his wings. Then he flew off Micki's shoulder and back into Puzzleworks.

"Sherlock hates fights," Alex explained.

At the end of the block a couple of kids were crossing the street at the intersection. A driver leaned out his car window. "What are you kids laughing at?"

"What?" asked a girl who must have been about 7 years old. She had half a candy bar in her mouth.

"You heard me. Now go on! Get out of my way before I run you down," the driver said.

The little girl started to cry. An older boy took her arm and hurried her across the street.

"Real friendly town you've got here, Alex," Micki said.

"Most of the time it is. Honest," Alex said. "Korina said you went to school here. You ought to know people don't usually act like this."

"I haven't really met that many people, I guess," Micki said. "We lived out in the country until Mom had to look for work. I hate living in our apartment." Then she seemed to cheer up. "So, where are we going now, Alex?"

"*We're* going to solve a mystery," Alex said, "*before* Korina and Christopher do."

"Great," said Micki. "What mystery?"

"The poison-p ..." Alex began. Then he remembered Detective Rule Number 7 about keeping Puzzle Club business private. "Sorry," he said. "I can't tell you."

"I understand," Micki said. "It's just that I can't be much help solving a mystery if I don't know what the mystery is."

"That's true," Alex said. After all, keeping the business private didn't mean he couldn't tell Micki *anything*. He just couldn't tell her *everything*. "It's about the letters," he said. "The mystery has to do with who's been sending certain letters."

Micki nodded. "What's in the bag?" she asked, pointing to the brown grocery bag in Alex's hand.

"That's my mail carrier disguise," he said proudly.

"That is so neat!" Micki said. "Where did you get it?"

Alex told Micki all about his disguises. She listened to his details about every disguise and thought his army and teacher disguises were especially clever. Micki was starting to make Alex think that maybe all 13-year-old girls weren't so bad after all.

"So what do we do now?" Micki asked.

"Now," Alex said, "I need to find somewhere to slip into my disguise."

Alex picked a big oak tree not far from Tobias' store. He pulled the uniform on over his clothes. Then he tugged the hat low over his eyes.

When Alex came out from behind the tree, Micki's eyes lit up. "Wow!" she said. "I almost didn't recognize you! You look exactly like a mail carrier."

Alex did feel like a mail carrier. But he felt like a detective too. If only Korina could see him as clearly as Micki did. "People should feel freer to talk about their letters with me if I'm in uniform," he explained.

"That's brilliant," Micki said. "I never would have thought of that, but it makes sense. Who's going to tell a regular person that somebody's calling them a cheat or fat or something. You're really good at this, Alex."

"Now we have to wait until the real mail carrier, Mr. Miller, finishes his long lunch and starts deliveries again."

They sat on the steps of the post office and kept a lookout for Mr. Miller. Alex found himself telling Micki all about Christopher and Korina. "Christopher is great," Alex said.

"He seemed nice," Micki agreed. "But do you think he knows what a good detective you are?"

Alex thought about it. Christopher sure *was* nice. But now that he thought about it, Christopher did usually take the big mystery assignments himself. And he counted on Korina to do most of the experiments.

"I don't know Korina that well," Micki said. "She's probably just having a bad day today."

"Korina acts like that all the time," Alex said. "She never takes me seriously as a detective."

Alex spotted Mr. Miller, the mailman, coming down the stairs. His big, leather mail pouch was slung over his shoulder. "There's the mailman," Alex said. "When Mr. Miller gets on his bike, we'll follow him. Then we can see if anybody else gets those letters."

"How will we know?" Micki asked.

"We'll know," he said.

Alex and Micki followed Mr. Miller as he rode his bike down the street and around the corner. At the first house, they hid behind a tree while he delivered the mail. Nobody was home so they continued to follow the bike.

At the third house, Mr. Miller handed three or four letters to an older woman Alex recognized, but he couldn't remember her name. She read the first letter and smiled.

"That's not it," Alex whispered.

The woman opened the next letter. She read it and let out a cry. "Albert!" she cried. "He would not dare!" She threw the letter down and ran inside the house.

Alex motioned to Micki to follow him to the porch. The letter lay faceup on the ground. It read: *Keep an eye on Albert. He doesn't love you anymore.*

That's who she was. Now Alex remembered. Mr. and Mrs. Albert Smith went to Alex's church. The note and paper looked just like the others Alex had seen.

Alex and Micki hurried to catch up with Mr. Miller. Out of the next four houses, only two people took their mail from the mailman. One, Mr. Walter, had just moved to town at the beginning of the year. It was his first year out of college. He taught gym at the middle school. The other person had a baby in one arm. It looked like she got a magazine and an envelope with a window in it. Probably a bill.

Alex and Micki climbed an oak tree so they could watch the next house safely. "Who lives there?" Micki asked.

"Mr. Bronson," Alex said. "He's really old. He talks to himself sometimes, but he's okay.

He used to run the gas station on Fourth Street. I think his son's got it now."

They watched as the old man looked at the only letter he was handed. He seemed almost shocked to get anything at all. As soon as Mr. Bronson opened the envelope, Alex knew. The letter was poison.

Mr. Bronson read his letter. His arm dropped to his side. Then, head hung low, he shuffled inside his house and closed the door.

"That must have been a poison-pen letter," Micki said.

"Come on," Alex said, jumping down from the tree. "Let's catch up with Mr. Miller." He took off running.

Alex kept running, but he looked back over his shoulder to see if Micki was following. That's when he ran smack into something. The first thing Alex saw as he fell backward was a shower of letters falling from the sky.

"Watch out!" yelled Mr. Miller. His bike tipped sideways, spilling him onto the street. Letters kept flying out of his bag. "What are you doing?" he cried. "Look where you're going!" The letters tumbled down the road.

"I'm sorry!" Alex said. He hustled to try and gather the letters. Micki came to the rescue and helped Alex pick up letters. She wiped off each letter before returning it to the mailbag.

"Micki," Alex whispered, "a bunch of these look like the same printing we saw on the poison-pen letters." Alex counted about 20 of them in the pile he picked up. He separated the poison-pen letters from the rest. "You really shouldn't deliver these," he told Mr. Miller.

"Give me those!" barked the mailman. "And where did you come up with that uniform?"

"At a garage sale," Alex said.

"Hmmmm. Well, I'm not sure," said Mr. Miller, "but it may be against the law to impersonate a mail carrier." He pushed the letters deep inside his bag and closed it.

Micki leaned over. "Why's he so crabby?" she whispered.

"Maybe he got a letter too," Alex said. Alex decided they'd followed the mail enough for one day. "Sorry again, Mr. Miller," he said as the mailman climbed back onto his bike. "Is there anything we can do to help?"

"The only thing you can do to help," said Mr. Miller, "is stop pretending to be a mailman. And stay out of my way!"

Alex slipped out of his uniform. He'd gotten pretty hot. "Micki," he said, "there's not much more we can do this afternoon. Want to sit in the shade until it's time to go to Tobias' for dinner?"

Alex and Micki backtracked to the town square and sat on one of the benches under a broad elm tree. Across the park, Alex heard angry voices. In the street, two drivers exchanged heated words. Alex pulled out his notepad and tried to write down every clue he could remember, including the names on the poisoned envelopes.

When Alex closed his notepad, Micki said, "Tell me more about Korina, Alex."

Alex started talking and couldn't stop. He told Micki how Korina always made fun of him, how she thought her ideas were great and his were stupid. "She's the one who doesn't know how to have fun," Alex said. "She's always so serious. I think part of it is because her parents thought something was wrong with her until she was about 5 years old. Korina didn't say a word until she was 4 years old. Of course, ever since then, she hasn't stopped talking."

Alex felt a small pang of guilt. He knew you weren't supposed to gossip about people. But this wasn't exactly gossip. And Korina wasn't exactly people.

Alex flipped open his notebook again. Micki peered over his shoulder. "What did you come up with this time, Alex?" she asked. "Do you know who wrote all those poison-pen letters yet? It would be great if you solved the case before Korina."

Alex wanted that too. He studied all the names and thought out loud. "How can anybody know so many people's weaknesses? It's like somebody could read their minds. And so many letters! Maybe there's more than one person. Maybe a bunch of people are writing letters." He felt his mind and heart racing now. He was close to an answer. He just knew it.

Mind reader. Mind readers. Nobody on earth could read minds. He thought of all those letters flying down at him as if they'd dropped from the sky. "That's it! I've got it!" he screamed. "I know who sent all those letters!"

"Who, Alex?" Micki asked.

Alex checked the sidewalk in both directions. Then he whispered the answer to the poison-pen mystery: "Aliens!"

5

Aliens, Schm-aliens

Alex hopped off the park bench. "I can't wait to see Korina's face when she finds out I solved the mystery before she did!"

Micki stood up and followed Alex out of the town square. "Korina will sure be surprised. She acted like she was the star detective. How did you figure out aliens wrote the letters, Alex?"

"It wasn't *that* hard," Alex said, trying to be modest. "I knew it had to be somebody—or something—that could read minds. Otherwise the writer wouldn't know what to write about everybody."

They crossed the street to Puzzleworks. "Alex," Micki said, "maybe you shouldn't tell Christopher and Korina just yet."

41

"Why?" Alex was ready to shout his success in Korina's face.

"Well," Micki said, "I don't know much about this detective business. But it seems to me, Korina might be the type to take your solution and pass off the idea as her own. You know, take the credit for herself?"

"You do have a point," Alex said. He imagined Korina announcing to Tobias and Mr. Randolph that *she'd* solved the mystery. It wouldn't be fair. "What do you think I should do?"

"Why don't you wait until we're having dinner. Then you can announce it to everybody. Korina can't take the credit then."

Alex agreed. Sherlock flew to his shoulder as soon as he and Micki stepped inside Puzzleworks. Tobias and Christopher were putting a red checked tablecloth over a table in the back of the store.

"Alex! Micki!" Tobias called. "I've brought everything from my house. I thought we'd have more fun if we ate here. What do you think, Alex?"

"Good idea, Tobias," Alex said. He looked around for Korina. "Where's Korina?" he asked.

"She's still at headquarters," Christopher said. He set red paper plates around the table.

"Korina is almost sure she's identified the paper used for the notes."

"Uh huh." Alex winked at Micki. It wasn't going to be easy waiting to tell everybody.

"I hope you solve this soon," Tobias said, setting out forks and knives. "You wouldn't believe how grouchy and angry my customers have been all day. I've never seen the town like this."

"I'm sure it will all be over soon," Alex said. He winked again at Micki.

Tobias put Alex and Micki to work filling water glasses and making salad. By the time Micki's grandfather arrived, they were ready to eat.

"Micki's mother couldn't make it," said Mr. Randolph. "She sends her thanks, but the mayor's wife called. They needed an emergency house cleaning."

Christopher yelled up the stairs for Korina. When she came down, she looked as if she'd just won the Nobel prize for science.

Everybody sat down. "You two kids have fun?" Korina asked Alex.

Alex bit his tongue to keep from answering.

Tobias said the blessing. "Bless this food we are about to eat, Lord. And thank You for bringing my good friend back to town. In Jesus' name. Amen."

"Tobias," said Mr. Randolph, helping himself to garlic bread. "You're a great cook. I have to admit though, the town isn't like I remember it. People used to be ... well ... friendlier, happier."

Tobias dropped his fork, splattering rigatoni sauce. "Randy, please don't judge the town by the way people are acting today. I've never seen ..."

"It's all right, Tobias," Mr. Randolph said. "I may have been wrong to think I could move back here."

Alex couldn't keep still another minute. "It's going to be okay," he said. "People are going to be able to get back to normal. I've solved the mystery!"

Silence covered Puzzleworks like a thick blanket. Alex looked around the table at the frowning, puzzled faces. Finally, Korina spoke. "*You've* solved the mystery?"

"Yes!" Alex insisted. "I know who's been sending the poison-pen letters. Aliens!"

Alex expected questions or congratulations. Instead, the faces around the table remained puzzled.

All at once Korina's laugh broke the silence. "Aliens?" She laughed so hard, she almost choked on her rigatoni. "That's a good one, even for you, Alex." She turned to Mr. Randolph. "You'll have to excuse Alex, Mr. Randolph. He has a bad habit of jumping to conclusions."

"It is too aliens!" Alex said. "I figured it out myself. They're the only ones who could read everybody's mind."

Korina gave Alex one of her pitying looks. "Poor Alex," she said. "And how did these *aliens* get hold of the mayor's stationery?"

Alex glared at her. Korina didn't know what she was talking about. She just couldn't stand seeing him get the credit for solving a case by himself. And why didn't Christopher stand up for him?

"No answer, Alex?" Korina asked. Then she turned to Tobias. "I've proven scientifically that the paper used to write our sample poison-pen letter came from the mayor's office. I matched it with the centennial invitations Christopher and I received."

"Okay," Alex said. "So maybe the aliens stole stationery from the mayor's office." He had to admit his solution was looking weaker and weaker. Still, Korina didn't have to make him look stupid in front of Micki and everybody.

"Aliens, schm-aliens," Korina said. "Admit it, Alex. You jumped to conclusions—again." She turned to Mr. Randolph. "Christopher and I keep telling Alex that if he wants to succeed with The Puzzle Club, he has to stop jumping to conclusions."

"Oh yeah?" Alex said. He pushed his chair back, making a loud scraping noise on the wood floor. Alex leaned across the table into Korina's face. "Well, you won't have to worry about poor Alex messing up your precious Puzzle Club investigations anymore. I quit!"

6

Suspicions and Suspects

Alex and Micki met at the library the morning after Tobias' dinner. "I think you did the right thing," Micki said. "Korina had no right to talk to you that way."

Alex had hardly slept all night. He didn't know what he'd do without The Puzzle Club. Chris-topher and Korina had been his friends for a long time.

"Come on, Alex," Micki said. "I've got to go work at the mayor's office. We're finishing up some stuff for the centennial celebration. Come with me."

Alex sighed and let Micki lead him down the walk toward city hall. Horns blared as drivers honked angrily. Two men were yelling across the street at each other. Alex didn't care about any of it.

"This will take your mind off The Puzzle Club," Micki said. They climbed the steps to the mayor's office. "You'll see."

The office was wild. People ran from the inner office to the outer one. Fax machines and printers roared. A dozen men and women sat at a big table, addressing envelopes. Phones rang and four secretaries dashed to answer them.

Alex didn't want to think about the case, but he couldn't help himself. If the notes were really written on stationery from the mayor's office, any one of these people could have done it.

The mayor greeted Alex and Micki at the door. "Don't just stand there," he said. "There's work to be done! I don't know what's gotten into everybody. We've had nothing but arguments all day."

As if on cue, a woman sprang up from the table. "What do you mean by that? There's nothing in my past that I'm ashamed of!" She stormed out of the office.

Alex recognized the mayor's wife talking on one of the phones. Micki joined the people at the long table and started licking envelopes. Alex decided to have a look around. He pulled out his notepad and wrote down his observations. He started by listing the names of the people in the office. Any one of them might have used the stationery.

Alex spent most of the day nosing around the mayor's office and getting nowhere. He still wanted to solve the mystery on his own and show Korina and Christopher he didn't need them. But how was he supposed to figure out who used the stationery to write poison-pen notes?

Then Alex got an idea. It just might work. "Everybody," he said, "could I have your attention?" Nobody paid attention to him.

Alex jumped up on top of the mayor's desk. "Could I please have your attention?" he shouted at the top of his lungs.

The room got quiet. "Alex, what are you …" the mayor began.

Alex stopped him. "Please, Mayor, just let me have a minute." He looked around at the sea of frowning faces. "I think we all know something bad's going on around town. Somebody's been sending poison-pen letters."

People looked down at their hands, cleared their throats, or looked away.

"I'm trying to find out who's sending the letters," Alex said. "But I need your help. Nobody but you will know what your letter said, but I need to know who got one. How many of you received a poison-pen letter?"

Alex wanted some way to narrow his list of suspects. He figured he could cross off the name of anyone who got a letter. "Please," he said. "It's important. Raise your hand if you got a poison-pen letter."

Just when Alex thought his plan had failed, he saw one hand slowly go up. It was Miss Jones. Alex thanked her and crossed off her name. Then another hand went up and another. Alex crossed names and more names off his list. Before Alex finished, every grown-up in that room—except the mayor and his wife—had raised a hand. Without a word, the volunteers stared at one another. Alex thanked them, hopped off the desk, and left.

He was out on the sidewalk before Micki caught up with him. "What do you make of that, Alex?" she asked.

Alex didn't know what to make of it. He was about to tell Micki he didn't have any conclusions when he spotted Christopher walking toward them.

"Alex," Christopher called, "wait up!" Christopher stopped in front of Alex and put a hand on his shoulder. "Alex," he said, "you left before I could talk to you last night. We …"

"You there! Puzzle Club!" The mayor came thundering up to them. Sweat dripped from his face. His tie hung loose around his neck. "What have you done to me, son?" he cried.

"Me?" Alex asked.

"Yes, you!" screamed the mayor. "All my volunteers have quit. They've walked out on me! I don't see how we can have the centennial celebration now. And why? All because I'm the only one who didn't receive some stupid poison letter! Thanks to you, I won't be giving the welcome speech at the centennial. If those people have their way, they'd rather see me lynched! You have made me the number 1 suspect in the poison-pen mystery!"

7

Poison Pain

"I admit the mayor likes his gossip," Tobias said. "But I can't see him writing poison-pen letters." Alex and Christopher had run straight from their sidewalk encounter with the mayor to ask Tobias for his advice. Micki went back with the mayor to his office to try and help out.

"It's my fault," Alex said. "Again. I guess I made everybody in his office think the mayor sent those poison-pen letters. I didn't mean to."

"Nonsense, Alex," Tobias said, coming around the front of his puzzle counter. "You've done nothing wrong. But I need The Puzzle Club. Some-body's got a grudge against this town. They're doing everything they can to see that this centennial celebration doesn't take place. In the meantime, a lot of people are being hurt." Tobias sighed deeply. "And I wanted everything to be perfect for my old friend."

"Has Mr. Randolph received a poison-pen letter yet?" Christopher asked.

"No, he hasn't, thank goodness," said Tobias.

The door to Puzzleworks burst open. Korina stormed into the room like a tornado.

"Korina," Christopher said, "what's the matter?"

Korina's eyes were filled with tears. She glared at Alex and wiped her eyes with the back of her hand. "You want to know what's the matter?" she asked, pushing past them. "Ask *him!*" She pointed at Alex.

"Christopher," Alex said, "will you please tell Korina I have no idea what she's talking about."

Before Christopher could carry out the request, Korina said, "And you can tell Alex for me that he's going to be sorry. Only one person could have sent this letter, and I'm going to prove it!" She shook the letter in her fist, pulled the gold cord, and ran up the stairs to Puzzle Club headquarters.

Tobias, Christopher, and Alex stared dumbfounded after Korina. Alex heard the code being punched in and the door to headquarters slam.

"She's been sent a poison-pen letter," Christopher whispered.

"But why did she say to ask me about it?" Alex asked. "That's not my fault too."

Tobias shook his head slowly. "The poison is spreading," he said. " 'The poison of vipers is on their lips.' That's what God's Word says about gossip and slander. And it says, 'The tongue also is a fire, a world of evil among the parts of the body … Brothers, do not slander one another.' This comes from the book of James."

"*Braawk! Fire!*" screeched Sherlock. He flew in circles around Puzzleworks.

Alex thought about the words. It was true that the words on those letters were like poison and like fire. They were blazing out of control through the town.

"I'll see to Korina," Tobias said. "Christopher, Alex, it's up to you to put out this fire."

Christopher and Alex left Puzzleworks together. "This doesn't mean I'm back with The Puzzle Club," Alex said.

"No, I understand," Christopher said.

It wasn't exactly the answer Alex had hoped to hear. "I mean, I really meant it when I quit," Alex said.

"And I'll respect that," Christopher said. "We'll work on this for Tobias. That's all."

Alex didn't know what else to say.

"Tobias may be right, you know," Christopher continued. "Somebody must have a grudge against the whole town. If only we knew who had received letters."

Alex pulled out his notepad. "That's part of my investigation," he said. He handed his notes to Christopher.

"Alex," Christopher said, "this is great! All these people got poison-pen letters?"

Alex felt pretty proud of his detective work. "Yep," he said. "I made this list from following Mr. Miller, the mailman, yesterday. And these are the volunteers at the mayor's office who received letters."

"Now that's funny," Christopher said, studying Alex's notes. "Except for the mayor's volunteers, everybody on this list is old—as old or older than Tobias."

Alex hadn't even thought of that, but Christopher was right. Miss Jones, Mr. and Mrs. Albert Smith, Mr. Bronson, Mr. Hales, Tobias.

"What do you think it means, Christopher?" he asked.

"It might mean that this grudge against the town goes way, way back. I think we'd better pay a little visit to the library."

8

Deadly Secrets

Alex sat in the basement of the library in front of the microfiche screen. Article after article from the town's newspaper whirred by in front of him.

"You stick with it down here, Alex," Christopher said. "It's close to closing time. I'll go talk to Mrs. Connolly, the librarian. She's lived here for 50 years. She might know who has a grudge against the town."

Alex watched headlines spin by until he felt dizzy. He hit the "stop" button. Just then the lights in the basement dimmed. "Christopher?" Alex called, his voice cracking. "Is that you?"

Nothing but the hum of the machine in front of him broke the silence of the basement. Alex looked from the dusty bookshelf to the piles of newspapers in the corner of the basement. He was all alone.

Alex heard a thud. A book bounced to the floor from a shelf behind him. "Is anybody there?" Alex called, his voice shaky. He thought he heard footsteps behind the stacks.

Alex tried to convince himself it was just his imagination. But his heart was pounding so hard, he had trouble listening to his head.

Alex heard a loud creak, then a high-pitched "*Ooooh!*" If he hadn't given up his alien theory, this would have been his proof. "Who's there?" Alex asked louder than before. Alex jumped up from his seat and made a mad dash for the stairs.

Smack! Alex slammed into somebody … or something. "Help!" he screamed. "Don't hurt me!"

"Alex?" It was only Christopher. "Where are you going? And why do you have the lights off?"

"Somebody turned off the lights," Alex explained. "Someone was down here watching me!"

Christopher found the switch and flipped the lights back on. "I don't see anybody, Alex." He walked over to where Alex had been sitting.

"Come on, Alex," he said. "What did you find out?"

Christopher sat down in front of the machine. Alex stepped cautiously behind him.

"Mrs. Connolly gave me a lead," Christopher said, "but she didn't want to drag it all up again. I could tell something was wrong. She didn't want to talk about it. But she did tell me I should check the newspapers from about 34 years ago."

Alex pressed the button and watched as the years went backward—20, 25, 30, 32, 33, 34 years.

"There!" Christopher said. "Go slow."

"What are we looking for?" Alex asked.

"I'm not sure," Christopher said, moving slowly through the front pages of the *Daily Record*. "Poison. Or something that would give somebody a grudge against ..." Christopher stopped.

Alex understood. They'd found the right headline. Alex and Christopher stared at each other in silence, then looked back at the article. On the screen was the face of a young man. Beneath the picture was the headline: *Randolph Goes to Prison for Stealing Town Blind!*

Christopher read the whole article aloud while Alex followed along. Tobias' friend, barely out of high school, had been caught with two other young men robbing Hales Market. The police uncovered stolen goods from every store in town. In the trial that followed, more than 40 people from the town—including Miss Jones—testified against Randy Randolph. As a result, he was found guilty and sentenced to 20 years in prison.

Alex stared at the picture of the young man. "Christopher," he said, "how are we ever going to tell Tobias that the poison-pen writer is his very own friend, Randy Randolph?"

9

Poison Past

It was pitch dark as Alex and Christopher left the library. Bright stars lit up the sky above the town square. "Can we wait until tomorrow to break the news to Tobias?" Alex asked as they stood on the library steps.

"We're still not sure we have the solution, Alex," Christopher said. "Let's sleep on it. We can talk to Tobias tomorrow. I don't know about you, but I'm going to pray about what to say to Tobias. I'll see you tomorrow morning. Night, Alex."

Alex walked home in the dark. The drivers that passed him seemed to be as angry as the drivers he'd seen honking and yelling all day. *The tongue is a fire,* Alex thought. *Poison.*

Alex was worried about telling Tobias about his friend. But something else troubled him as he crossed the street and reached his own block. Korina had been wrong about him. He hadn't written her poison-pen letter. But he had done his own brand of poison. He'd said some pretty mean things about Korina. He'd told Micki that Korina was too bossy. He'd called Korina a know-it-all. If he wanted to stop the poison in the town, maybe he was going to have to start with himself.

The porch light was on at his house, and Alex heard the blur of voices from the TV. He said goodnight to his parents and went up to bed. The moon sent its light through Alex's window. As he said his prayers before he dropped off to sleep, Alex asked Jesus for help. "Help me to forgive people who are mean to me just like You did," he said, drifting to sleep. "And please, no more poison. No more poison."

Early the next morning, Alex met Christopher by the front door to Puzzleworks. Across the street, Rafferty's big centennial banner flapped against the tree. A wood platform stood at the other end of the park. So much trash lay across the lawn, Alex wondered if people had thrown it there on purpose.

"Are you ready, Alex?" Christopher asked.

Alex shrugged. For the second night in a row, he hadn't slept well. His head felt cloudy and his heart heavy. But he followed Christopher through the front door of Puzzleworks. He knew they'd have to tell Tobias what they'd found out about Mr. Randolph.

Christopher stopped so suddenly inside Puzzleworks that Alex ran into the back of him. Sherlock flew to Christopher's shoulder, then hopped to Alex's. Alex peeked around to see not only Tobias but Randy Randolph.

"Don't just stand there," Tobias called. "I've been filling Mr. Randolph in on the poison-pen puzzle. Have you come up with any more clues?"

Christopher had opened his mouth to answer when Korina and Micki walked into the store.

"And where have you girls been?" asked Mr. Randolph.

"Micki and I had a good talk about *my* note," Korina said. She turned to Alex. "Alex, I thought you were the one who sent it to me."

"I didn't, Korina!" Alex said.

"I know that now," Korina said. "Last night I did tests on the notes. It was sent by the same person who wrote all the other notes. Even I couldn't believe you'd done that. Then this morning Micki showed up to convince me that you didn't write it. So I guess I'm ... sorry."

Korina said the last word so softly, Alex wasn't sure he'd heard her. He should have felt better, but he didn't.

"Korina," Alex said, "I didn't write poison words but I did say them. I've said some pretty mean things about you in the last couple of days."

Alex turned to Micki. "Micki could tell you. I griped a lot about you to her. What I'm trying to say is that I'm sorry. Poison is poison, whether you write it or say it behind somebody's back."

Korina didn't say anything. Then she grinned at Alex, crossed the room to stand in front of him, and stuck out her hand. Alex shook Korina's hand.

"Welcome back to The Puzzle Club," Korina said.

"You mean it?" Alex asked.

"We can't solve this case without you," said Korina.

The case. Alex had almost forgotten why they were there. They still had to warn Tobias about Mr. Randolph. And what about Micki? What would she do when she learned what her grandfather really was?

"Speaking of the case," Tobias said, "you were about to tell me what you found out."

Alex waited for Christopher. Christopher shifted his weight from one foot to the other. Finally, he blurted it out. "Tobias, we're sorry to have to tell you this. But the only one we could find who might have a grudge against the town ... is Mr. Randolph."

Alex saw Mr. Randolph and Tobias exchange wide-eyed looks. He glanced at Micki, but she was staring at her grandfather.

"That will be enough of that, Christopher," Tobias said sternly.

"But Tobias," Alex said, "Christopher's just telling you what we found out. You need to know. It happened 34 years ago. Mr. ..."

But Tobias cut Alex off. "That's enough, Alex!" he said. "I will not hear one word against my friend. And that's final."

"But ..." Alex began.

This time it was Christopher who stopped him. "He knows," Christopher whispered. "Tobias knows all about it."

Of course, Alex thought. Tobias must be about the same age as Randy Randolph. He knew all along about his friend's prison record.

"Well, would somebody please inform me as to what is going on around here?" Korina asked. "What are we not talking about? What about 34 years ago?"

"Absolutely nothing to do with this case, Korina!" Tobias said firmly. "Now I want everybody here to forget ..."

"No, Tobias," said Mr. Randolph quietly. "Forgetting isn't the answer."

"No, Grandpa!" Micki yelled. She ran up and hugged his waist. Then she shot Alex and Christopher hateful glares. "They think *you* did it," she said. "They think they're so smart for finding out what happened."

"How did you know what we discovered?" Christopher asked.

Alex thought about the lights going off in the library basement. Micki knew her way around the library. Korina had said so. That squeal Alex had heard in the library. Maybe it hadn't been his imagination. Maybe it had been Micki.

"I've paid my dues, Micki," said her grand-father. "I'd like the chance to explain." He turned to Tobias. "Tobias, you've been a good friend. You haven't said one word about my past since I've come back. I appreciate that more than you'll know."

Tobias nodded his head. Then he made everyone sit in his puzzle corner so Mr. Randolph could tell his story.

"I was just a kid," Mr. Randolph began, "a punk who thought he was smarter than the whole town. I fell in with the Barstow brothers, and they were a bad lot. We started out taking things from Hales Market—first gum and candy, then bigger things. It seemed more like a game than anything else. We took petty cash from the Laundromat, then rings from the jewelry store. Before long, we'd robbed every store around here."

"You don't have to go through this again," Tobias said.

"I want to, Tobias. Well, the Barstow boys got an idea. They didn't tell me about it until it was too late. To be honest, I'm not sure what I would have done if they had told me. They drove me to Bronson's gas station on the high-way. Then they told me to pretend I had a gun.

I was to see if I could get the attendant, Albert Smith, to give up some cash."

Alex remembered Albert Smith and his wife. They'd gotten a poison-pen letter. So had Mr. Hales. And Mr. Bronson. If anything, Alex was more convinced than ever that they'd found the poison-pen writer.

Randy Randolph continued his story. "Well, I burst into that gas station and pretended to have a gun. But the Barstow brothers didn't pretend. The older boy had a real gun.

"We got caught and convicted of armed robbery. I was sent to jail. My boy, Micki's father, died while I was in prison. I couldn't face anybody after I got out, so I took a job in South America. I've come back now to make up for it."

"To get revenge?" Korina asked. "With poison-pen letters?"

"Korina!" Tobias scolded. "You're jumping to conclusions. First you accuse Alex and now Mr. Randolph."

Alex liked having somebody else jump to conclusions for a change. But something was nagging at him. "Korina," Alex said, "what made you think I sent you your poison-pen letter? I mean, I know we were mad at each other, but that's not enough reason to make you think I sent it."

"I thought you might have sent just one poison letter, mine. I didn't think I was jumping to conclusions either. As far as I knew, nobody but you—and my mother—knew the things that were in my letter."

"What, Korina?" Alex asked. "What was in your letter?"

Korina looked away. For a minute Alex was sure she wasn't going to tell him what her poison-pen letter said. Then she let it out. "It said everybody knew I wasn't so smart because I didn't talk until I was 4 years old."

"Even *I* didn't know that," Christopher said.

"I know," Korina said. "I never told that to anybody ... except Alex."

"Well, I never wrote it," Alex said. "And I never told anybody ... except Micki."

All eyes turned toward Micki. She had been sitting perfectly still next to her grandfather. Suddenly, she jumped up. With tears streaming down her cheeks, she screamed at them. "Yes! I did it! It was me! I wrote the letters."

10

The Antidote: Overcoming Evil with Good

"Micki, what are you saying?" asked her grandfather.

"I did it for you, Grandpa. Because this town ruined your life! It kept you from us and made all of our lives miserable."

"But how did you know so much about so many people?" Alex asked. He knew he'd griped about Korina. But he couldn't have passed on information about everybody in town.

"I knew a little bit from things I'd heard my folks say. But as soon as I volunteered at the mayor's office, I heard more than enough gossip to go around."

That explained it. Alex remembered how full of gripes the mayor had been in Tobias' store that first day he'd met Micki. Then another thing clicked. Alex remembered when he and Micki had followed Mr. Miller, the mailman. Micki had said, "Who's going to tell a regular person that somebody's calling them a cheat or fat or something?" But Alex had never told her what the letters said. She already knew because she'd written them. How had he missed that clue?

Mr. Randolph reached out and pulled his granddaughter toward himself. "Micki, Micki," he said. "It wasn't the town's fault, girl. What I did, I did to myself. I was the one who stole."

"But they robbed you of all those years," she said, sobbing.

"I won't lie to you. Those years in prison were horrible. I wouldn't wish them on another soul. But something happened to me in prison, Micki. Something that made it all worth it. God used my time in prison to show me what true freedom is."

"I don't understand," Micki said.

"I had a lot of time on my hands in prison and not much to read. A pastor visited me one day and gave me a Bible. I read it, and I learned that God offers us freedom in Jesus. I didn't have to go around feeling guilty my whole life.

Jesus paid for my sins when He died on that cross. I don't have a grudge against anyone, Micki, and neither should you. I'm thankful God reached me—even if I did have to go to prison to learn about His freedom."

"I've wanted to tell you the whole story for a long time, Tobias," said Mr. Randolph. "I've thought often about how you loved God, even back then."

Puzzleworks door flew open. The mayor stepped inside. "Well, I'm glad you're all having such a cozy time," he said. "That's the last time I ask The Puzzle Club for help!"

"Mayor?" said Tobias. "What's wrong? What's happened?"

"Everybody in this town has gone mad! I was taking my life into my own hands just walking over here," the mayor said. "The centennial celebration is canceled. The way things are going, this whole town will be canceled!"

Tobias took the mayor into the back room and tried to calm him down. Meanwhile, Christopher, Korina, and Alex put their heads together.

"How can we get the people in this town back to the way they used to be?" Korina asked. "I've never seen the town act like this. It's as if the whole town has been poisoned."

"How can we stop everybody from being mad?" Alex asked. He wasn't about to say it, but it scared him to think about living in a town where people didn't like one another.

"I have an idea," said Christopher. He squinted as if his brain were squeezing the idea together.

"What is it?" asked Mr. Randolph. "Can I help?"

Micki didn't say anything, but she stared at Christopher.

"There's only one way to fight evil," Christopher said. "Overcome evil with good. It's the antidote to poison."

"Huh?" Alex asked.

"We'll have to work really hard. I'll need all the help I can get," Christopher said.

"I'm in!" Korina and Alex said it at exactly the same moment.

"Count me in," said Mr. Randolph.

Christopher led the way to Puzzle Club headquarters. Mr. Randolph followed him. Then Korina. Then Alex.

"Psst!" Alex turned. Micki peered up at him with sad, reddened eyes. "Alex," she said. "Can I help too?"

11

The Power
of a Good Word

For the next eight hours, neither Christopher, Korina, Alex, Mr. Randolph, nor Micki set foot outside Puzzle Club headquarters. Neither did Sherlock, who flew from person to person, watching the flurry of activity.

Piles of paper and envelopes littered the examination table. Alex used the phone book to address envelopes. Everybody else wrote as fast as they could.

"What should I write to Miss Jones?" Micki asked, chewing on her pencil eraser. She was sitting on a pillow in front of the window that overlooked Main Street. Through the open window came the angry voices of two women arguing.

"Say something about how it's no secret what a wonderful teacher she is and always has been," Alex suggested. "And tell her that one student will never forget the time he misspelled *good*. He spelled it *g-o-d*, but she wouldn't let the other kids laugh at him. Instead she said he was smart to know that God was good."

"Neat, Alex," Micki said, writing quickly.

Alex caught a glimpse of some of the other letters as he stuffed them into envelopes. Christopher had written one to Mr. Hales about how fair he was with his prices and how the town would hate it if he went out of business. Mr. Randolph wrote a nice one to Albert Smith and his wife. He said how great it was that they set such a good example of a loving married couple. The town counted on them to be good examples.

"Do you really think these letters are going to do any good?" Micki asked.

"Honey," said her grandfather, "if God's goodness could reach through all that evil in prison, I think it ought to reach here."

It was late by the time Alex licked the last envelope shut.

"That's it," said Christopher. He divided the envelopes and handed each person a stack. "If we deliver the letters ourselves, people can get them first thing in the morning. It might not be too late to pull off this centennial celebration after all."

Alex delivered his letters by the light of a full moon. Nobody was out around town celebrating so nobody stopped to ask him what he was doing.

Alex could hardly keep his eyes open, but he had one more thing to do. He pulled out a sheet of paper and wrote one last note.

Alex woke up, rolled over, and stared at his clock. It was almost 10 A.M.! He dressed, gobbled down breakfast, and raced outside.

"Good morning, Alex," came a cheerful voice from the sidewalk.

Alex turned and was surprised to see Miss Jones' smiling face. "Good morning, Miss Jones," he said.

"And isn't it just the most beautiful morning?" she said, beaming at him. "Listen to that bird sing. That's a goldfinch, Alex."

"Yes, Miss Jones," Alex said, amazed at the change in his old teacher.

"Mr. Webb!" Miss Jones hollered at the old man across the street. "Just a minute. I'll help you with that." She said good-bye to Alex and crossed the street to help Mr. Webb with his bags of groceries.

Alex walked half a block before he heard loud voices ahead of him. This time the noise was laughter. Two couples stood in the middle of the road, laughing out loud. Drivers, instead of honking and yelling out of their windows at them, smiled and drove carefully around the group.

By the time Alex reached the town square, he'd witnessed 14 handshakes, six hugs, and a kiss. He'd lost count of the number of hellos and how-are-yous. The square was filled with crowds of people. Kids played on the slides and swings. Little groups of men and women laughed and talked together. They called out greetings to people as they passed.

The mayor climbed his platform and cleared his throat in front of the microphone. Alex spotted Korina and Christopher toward the front of the crowd. When he got closer, he saw Tobias and Mr. Randolph too.

"Isn't it amazing?" Korina said.

"Everybody's so nice," Alex said. "Can you believe it?" He looked around. "Where's Micki?"

"We haven't seen her today," Christopher said.

"Look!" Korina said. "There she is."

Alex looked toward the speaker's platform where Korina was pointing. There stood Micki, right behind the mayor.

"Ladies and gentlemen," said the mayor, "if I could please have your attention. I'd like to introduce someone to you."

"What's Micki doing up there?" Alex asked Mr. Randolph.

"I have no idea, Alex," said Mr. Randolph.

"This is Micki Randolph," said the mayor. "I'm not exactly sure what she has to say. She only asked this morning if she could say a few words. Micki was my hardest working volunteer on this centennial celebration, so I had to say yes." He smiled and laughed a little. "Go ahead, Micki."

Micki stepped up to the microphone. She pulled the mike down to her level. "I-I-I just want to tell everyone I'm sorry," she said.

The crowd turned to one another and shrugged.

"I'm the one who wrote those awful poison-pen letters," she said.

"You?" came a voice from the crowd.

"Why, how dare you!" came another voice. Murmurs and grumblings broke out all across the town square. For a minute, Alex was afraid all the good feelings of the day had left.

"Please," she said, "please listen to me."

Eventually the crowd noise died down enough so Micki could be heard.

"Why I did it doesn't really matter," Micki said. "It was wrong. And I'm so sorry. That's why I asked the mayor to let me speak. I wanted to apologize to everybody."

Nobody said anything. Alex wasn't at all sure they were ready to accept Micki's apology. He jumped up on the first step of the platform. Then he shouted to the crowd in his loudest voice, "Micki helped write the *good* letters you got too!"

"She did?" came a voice.

"Well, I'll be," said another.

"Seeing all of you this morning—so happy and nice to each other," Micki said, "it's taught me that The Puzzle Club was right. Good *is* stronger than evil because God's love is stronger than anything." Micki stopped. Then she left the microphone and crossed the speaker's platform toward Alex.

Not a sound was heard in the town square except a goldfinch. Then Alex heard one single clap. Then another. And another. And before Micki reached the steps of the platform, the whole town square broke out in thunderous applause. People shouted and cheered and laughed. They gave each other high-fives and hugs.

"Well, I'll be," said the mayor, retaking the mike. "I don't imagine there will be another centennial like this one for at least 100 years!"

It was quite a celebration. And before Alex left that evening, he took something out of his pocket and handed it to Korina.

"What's this?" she asked, taking the letter Alex held out.

Alex kept quiet while Korina read. It had taken him a long time to write, but he'd recorded everything good he could think to write about Korina.

When Korina finished her letter, she reached out and hugged Alex. "Thanks, Alex," she said. "I suppose you're not such a bad detective yourself. Welcome back to The Puzzle Club!"